anythink

DISNEY

INF IN ITY

randomhousekids.com

For more information on Disney Infinity, please visit:
Disney.com/Infinity

ISBN 978-0-7364-3327-3 (trade)
ISBN 978-0-7364-8173-1 (lib. bdg.)

Printed in the United States of America

10 9 8 7 6 5 4 3 2 1

DISNEP

INF IN ITY

TREASURE HUNT!

By Amy Weingartner
Illustrated by Fabio Laguna and James Gallego

Random House New York

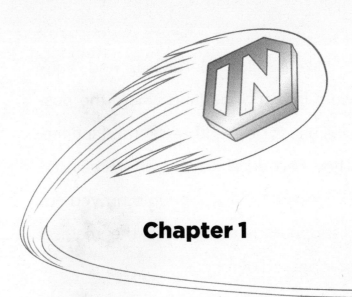

Chapter 1

"Captain Jack Sparrow, at your service," the pirate said. He bowed to Mike, a one-eyed green monster and his big blue friend, Sulley. "You say you found a treasure map?"

Mike and Sulley nodded.

Mike, Sulley, Barbossa, and Jack were in a strange land where the possibilities for adventure seemed infinite. They had each arrived after seeing a shooting star. New people arrived—or disappeared—every time the magical star passed overhead.

Jack and Barbossa had recently met a queen who could create ice and snow, a girl who drove a candy race car, and many other wonderful characters.

They had even fought a sinister villain named Syndrome and his army of robots.

They had been looking forward to going home when they'd met the two monsters . . . who claimed to have a treasure map.

"Forgive Jack for not introducing me. I'm Captain Barbossa."

"Another pirate captain!" said Mike. "Impressive. I'll be a captain. Captain Mike! Or I will be one day! I've always wanted to sail the seas and hunt for treasure. Although I do get seasick, which could be a problem. Luckily, I am already green."

They all gathered around the torn treasure map.

"It's difficult to read," said Jack. "And part of it is missing."

"Yeah," the green monster replied,

"but I think it says to go to a place called Agra—bara—bara—something."

Jack smiled. "Agrabah!" he said. "I know the place well. My ship is nearby. To Agrabah!"

"*My* ship," growled Barbossa.

Jack looked up to the sky, pondering how he might get rid of Barbossa. Just then, another shooting star appeared. Jack whispered to Mike, "See that star? Mesmerizing, wouldn't you say?"

"Wow!" said Mike. "Hey, Barbossa, look at that thing!"

Barbossa looked up and felt the star's pull. He started to resist it. "The blasted thing is calling me away. You won't find the treasure without me!"

"We'll try our best," said Jack as Barbossa disappeared in a swirl of magic stardust.

Before Mike and Sulley could react, they heard the *clop-clop* sound of approaching hooves. Across the terrain they saw what looked like a wild wave of red hair riding a swift horse. Jack drew his sword.

"Protect the map!" shouted Mike. He quickly buried it in Sulley's fur.

Jack pulled a spyglass out of his vest and peered into it. "It's a fair maiden!" he reported.

She rode up to the group but kept

her distance. "You sure *look* like a bunch o' troublemakers."

Sulley stepped forward. "Gee, miss, I would hate for you to think that. We're just on an important mission here."

"What *kind* of mission?"

"It's a secret," said Mike. "Come on, fellas, let's go. We don't need any more partners, right?"

"Partners? I'm new here, so count me in," the girl said.

At that moment, the map fell out of Sulley's fur. It rolled onto the ground and opened.

"Ooh! A treasure map!" The girl leapt off her horse, Angus, and read the map. "Hmmm," she said. "I see."

"*What* do you see?" said Mike, jumping up and down.

"So you're heading to a very, very dangerous part of the world, then?"

"Dangerous?"

"Well, it says right here the treasure be in the wild and dangerous Agrabah—"

"We knew that," said Jack.

"You can read it?" Mike said. "I'm Captain Mike, and I'm in charge of this treasure mission. You're in."

"I'm Merida," she said as she shook his hand before turning to her horse. "Angus, we're going on an adventure!"

Chapter 2

As they headed toward the ship, Jack saw something in the distance. "Villains! Prepare to defend yourselves!"

They ran along the shore as a group of pirates attacked from behind.

"Yikes!" Mike said.

"*This* happens more often than you might think," Jack replied.

"And *this* is what I call *adventure!*" Merida said. She pulled out her bow and arrows and began shooting at the pirates.

Jack Sparrow's *Black Ship* was docked just ahead. Merida and Sulley held off the pirates while Jack and Mike ran aboard the ship and prepared for launch.

Jack started to untie the ropes, but Mike ran to the ship's wheel. He was excited to be a pirate.

"Avast or whatever!" Mike said, pretending to be captain. "I'm going to sail this thing, and we are going to find *treasure*!"

"Wait!" Jack shouted. He raced over and took command of the wheel. "Mike, my good man. This is not a toy."

"Well, actually, it might be," said Mike. "A lot of things around here are toys." He held up a paintball gun. "Like

this thing. It just came out of nowhere, and it's mine now."

Jack pushed the paintball gun aside. "Everyone, all aboard. Now!"

Sulley, Merida, and Angus fought off the last of the pirates and ran aboard.

"Ready to lift anchor!" said Mike.

"Okay, Captain Mike," said Jack, "let's see what you can do."

The ship lurched as Mike, with Jack's help, steered them out of the bay. "I'm a natural!" Mike said.

"We have no time to lose—and treasure to find!" said Jack.

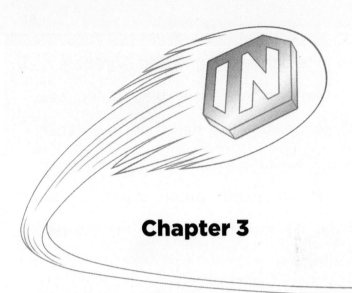

Chapter 3

They docked the *Black Ship* in a cove

lined with palm trees and rocks, where

lizards basked in the sun. The treasure

hunters traveled on foot across uneven

terrain and soon came upon a desert.

They crossed the sandy dunes, ready

to face danger . . . and find Agrabah.

"Any minute now, we should see large beasts—like half man, half leopards," said Merida, reading the map.

"Do they eat green things?" said Mike. He moved closer to his big pal, Sulley.

Just then, Jack spotted a creature darting from the shade of a palm tree. "Look out," he whispered, and brandished his sword.

The figure had a curly tail and many feet. As they got closer, the creature scampered right up to Mike and Sulley.

"Hiya, old pals," the creature said. "What are *you* doing here?"

"Randy!" Sulley said.

"Boy, are we glad to see you!" said Mike, giving him a giant hug.

"Really? I have *never* heard that from anyone!" said Randy.

"We thought maybe you were a half man, half leopard," said Mike.

"So you're not really glad to see *me*?

Then what are you doing here? And what's that?" Randy tore the map from Merida's hand. "Aha," he said, studying the paper. "The famous treasure of Agrabah! Count me in!"

"Gee, Randy," said Sulley. "We already have a few partners here."

"Yeah, we have to stay lean," said Mike.

"Lean and mean," said Randy. "I get it. Don't need Randy around, stinking up the place."

"No one said you stink," said Mike.

"You haven't seen the last of me!" Randy turned the color of sand and disappeared.

"Back on course—to the fair city of Agrabah!" said Jack.

Before long, the sand dunes ended and they were at the city's edge. They passed through the tall white gates of Agrabah and entered a market-place. Jack, Merida, Mike, and Sulley hid behind some carts to watch a big fight that was going on. It was hard to tell who were the good guys and who were the bad guys.

"Look over there," said Sulley. "That guy wearing the pajamas."

"And the wee vest and hat?" said Merida.

"He's quite a fighter," said Sulley.

They watched as the boy dodged the sword blows of a dozen Palace Guards.

"I got a feeling he's our map guy," said Mike, jumping into the fight. "Excuse me, I can see you're busy—"

The boy nodded and tossed Mike a sword.

"Okay, wow. All right! Take that! And *that*!"

"I'm Aladdin."

"I'm Mike. Oh no, incoming." Mike paused to attack one of the guards. "My friends and I have come a long way. We have a treasure map. You may have the other piece of it?"

"*Shhhh.* Keep it down," said Aladdin.

"These guards have heard of the map. They want it for themselves. They will try to block our way to my friend Jasmine. If anyone can help us find the treasure, it is surely her."

Aladdin and Mike were arguing on the steps of a huge white palace with towers. Palace Guards blocked their way.

"If your friends help me," Aladdin said, "I can take you to Jasmine."

Mike called the rest of the team and they came over. He introduced them to Aladdin as they helped drive back the guards.

Jack jumped on a nearby elephant.

The guards scattered to avoid being trampled.

Sulley used his roar-and-smash tactics to scare and demolish the guards. With a big roar, he smashed a barrel . . . and an oversized tricycle and a paintball gun appeared! He jumped onto the tricycle and rode circles around the guards, firing paintballs at them. The balloons popped, covering the guards with sticky paint.

Aladdin yelled to Sulley, "Cover us!"

Jack and Sulley continued to fight the guards. Aladdin slipped into his prince outfit and sneaked down an alley with Merida and Mike.

Aladdin pointed to the tower room where Jasmine lived. It was five stories above them.

"You know a shortcut to get up there?" asked Mike.

"I do," said Aladdin with a smile. He was looking at some carpets hanging on a line. He grabbed one of them and it began to sparkle.

They held on tight as they flew up the side of the tall tower.

"Aladdin!" Jasmine said when they reached the top. "Who are your friends?"

"My name's Merida. I like how you travel around here!" The fiery-haired girl jumped into the room. "We've

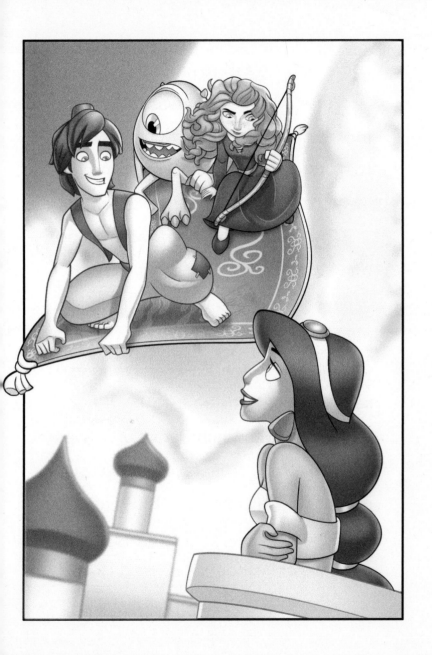

come with a treasure map!"

"I'm Mike. Nice to meet you. Let's put the map together right now," he said. "We should memorize it in case something happens to the pieces."

"The wee green one has a good point," said Merida.

They rolled out the map, and Jasmine put her map piece next to it.

"It leads to the Cave of Wonders," said Jasmine. "It's said to be a huge mountain with hundreds of caves underneath it. The mountain is surrounded by lava beds. But I thought it was a legend."

"Cave of Wonders it is," said Mike.

"It's not that simple," said Aladdin gravely. *"It will be treacherous."*

"But we're going," said Merida.

"You bet we are!" said Mike.

They jumped onto the carpet and swooped down to the ground. Just as the carpet landed, two newcomers greeted them near the palace steps.

"Oh, hello, my old school chum," said Randy to Mike. "Meet my new friend, Davy." The monstrous pirate glared down at Mike.

Davy Jones towered over the short monster, casting a dark shadow. Randy asked, "You know what Davy is? A pirate. You know what pirates like?"

Davy leaned down and wagged a tentacle at Mike.

"C-c-candy?" asked Mike innocently.

"Treasure," Randy said.

"*Your* treasure," the octopus-faced pirate growled.

Chapter 4

As soon as Jack saw the monstrous Davy Jones, he attacked. Now the marketplace was in a bigger uproar than before. Aladdin, Jasmine, Jack, Merida, Sulley, and Mike were fighting Randy, Davy, *and* the Palace Guards.

"Watch out!" shouted Sulley. One of the guards tried to grab Jasmine.

Then suddenly, a stranger—stranger than the monsters and sea demons already in the market—entered the fight. He was blue and looked like a rabbit with big teeth.

"Rrrrgh!" he roared. His paintball gun turned the guards a different color every time he fired.

"Nifty work, and so colorful," said Mike. "Let me see that thing. You know, I had one just like it a little while ago."

The creature, whose name was Stitch, turned to Mike and blasted him.

"Help me, I'm pink!" Mike cried,

covered in pink paint.

"Whose side are you on, anyway?" Merida asked the stranger.

"Stitch's side," Stitch said, and turned her yellow.

While Mike was cleaning off the paint from Stitch's paintball blast, a roar of engines filled the air. Davy and Randy rode by on motorcycles. Davy grabbed Mike.

Then Randy shoved Mike into his cycle's sidecar. They raced out the city gates with sand flying behind them and were gone before anyone could stop them.

"We've got to rescue Mike!" shouted

Sulley, worried about his friend.

"Now's our chance," said Merida. Stitch seemed to be fighting everyone . . . and having a great time doing it! While the guards were occupied, Jack worked out a plan with Jasmine and Aladdin.

"They must be headed to the Cave of Wonders," Jasmine said. "They have Mike *and* his map."

She raised her hands and spun them around. As she did, a cyclone of sand began to form and whirl in the air. Stitch and all the guards in the marketplace were caught up in its power and couldn't move. "Go and find Mike! I'll

keep the guards back as long as I can!"

"I hate to leave you behind," said Aladdin. "But we'll be quick."

"We have to be," said Jack. "I know Davy Jones. *Mike doesn't have much time.*"

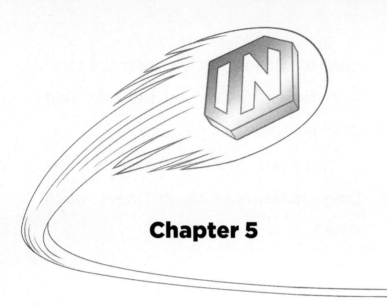

Chapter 5

The team crossed the deep sands of Agrabah by elephant, and soon they came to a rocky area with a mountain surrounded by many lava beds. They took out Jasmine's part of the map.

"The cave entrance should be

somewhere in that big wall of rock,"
said Aladdin, pointing.

They left Angus and the elephants
by a stream and went on foot toward
the rock wall. As they got closer, they
saw a huge tiger head carved in stone.

"Hey, look at that head—it's *way*
taller than me," said Sulley. The tiger's
mouth was open wide. To go into the

Cave of Wonders, they would have to step over the teeth and walk down its throat! It was terrifying, but they did it.

Inside, they looked around the empty stone room—no one was there. Jack disappeared into the shadows. In the corner, they noticed a green hand moving.

"Mike, old buddy!" Sulley called, and he ran across the room. It was Jack holding up a big floppy green hand.

Merida gasped. "They cut Mike to pieces!"

"Shhh," said Jack. "It's not the hand of Mike. But it does have bewitching powers. Look what happens."

Jack waved the hand and the walls moved. The floor opened to reveal stairs and a long path. Everyone ran down the stairs to the wall at the end of the path.

Aladdin got there first. When he touched the wall, it slid open and a golden lamp appeared. "The magic lamp!" he said. It lit up and sparkled, and it seemed to lead them into a door-lined tunnel below.

"There must be dozens of doors," Merida said. "Davy and Randy could be hiding Mike anywhere."

Then they heard a voice. "Sulley?"

They followed the voice to a door.

Through a set of jail bars they could see Mike stuck inside the mouth of a tiki statue that was ten feet tall! His arms were tied with long ropes attached to rings on the ceiling. The room was a narrow dungeon made of rock walls with a very high ceiling.

"You found me!" he said. "Now get me outta here!"

The door was locked. Aladdin held up his lamp. A swirl of light came out of the lamp and the door opened. "It's mainly good for doors," he said.

"How are we going to untie Mike?" asked Sulley. "The ceiling is way too high for us to get up there."

"Leave it to me," said Merida. She shot through the ropes holding Mike with an arrow. He tumbled out of the tiki statue.

"Oh, that feels much better," he said. "Now listen, the bad news is they took the map."

"Oh no!" said Merida.

"But I know where the treasure is— that's the good news. However, we also need the other half of *this*!" Mike held out his hand. In it rested a small, shiny object. It was molded from gold.

They leaned in and looked closer. "It's a mystical scarab beetle," Mike said. "You know, a magical dead bug."

Jack jumped back.

"Afraid of bugs, are ya?" Merida asked.

"Only when it is the ancient cursed mystical scarab beetle," Jack replied, making a face at the beetle.

"The legend," said Aladdin, "is that you must have both parts of the scarab to use its power. That's only half."

"Exactly," said Mike. "I heard ol' squidface and Randy talking. They had both halves. But I cleverly managed to switch one half with a chocolate cookie."

"They'll be back for it," said Aladdin.

"Where *is* the treasure?" asked Jack.

"Somewhere in this Cave of Wonders place. So we need the map back.
And we have to find those bad guys.
But at least I have the beetle," Mike
said triumphantly.

Chapter 6

Mike led the team out of the tunnel and up a dark, twisting staircase lit by torches. When they got outside, a big guy with a hammer-shaped head came up and drop-kicked Mike toward a lava bed. Sulley caught him in the air.

"Hey, cut that out," Sulley said. "Pick on someone your own size."

"We plan to," said Davy Jones, coming up behind them with Randy.

"Let's go!" shouted Jack.

Davy and Randy chased them to the edges of the red-hot molten lava beds. Long rope bridges hung across the lava.

"We can't go any farther!" Merida yelled.

"We have to make it across on foot," Jack replied.

One by one, the good guys crossed the rope bridges. They raced into the leafy green jungle on the other side.

"Watch out!" shouted Sulley. Huge mallets swung at them out of nowhere.

Randy tackled Mike as the gigantic mallets moved threateningly over their heads—*whoosh*—while they fought.

"I never"—*whoosh*—"expected you to be such a giant pain in the eyeball!" said Mike.

Whoosh. "That was your mistake!" *Whoosh.*

Suddenly, Stitch swung toward Mike on a vine and blasted him with bright blue paint.

Blue Mike tripped and fell over. The scarab beetle rolled away from him.

"*Ah-ha-ha-ha!*" Randy said, and he

grabbed the gold scarab. "Like my new bad-guy laugh?"

Then he blended in with the green leaves and was gone.

Jack, Merida, and Sulley ran over. "What happened?" Sulley asked.

"Stitch. Blue paint. Randy. Beetle. Gone. There goes our treasure."

Aladdin rode up on a horse. "We've got some friends. Look who's here!"

Mike wiped blue paint from his eyes and looked at a young black-haired superhero. He looked tough but friendly.

"My name is Hiro," the boy said.

"Good, we need a hero," said Mike.

"Look up!" said Aladdin. A robot in a red metallic supersuit flew in and landed next Hiro. *And* he was carrying Jasmine on his back!

She jumped down. "This is Baymax, everyone." Jasmine looked at Aladdin. "Kind of an upgrade from a carpet, don't you think?"

Chapter 7

Baymax was also a nurse bot. He bent over Mike. "You appear to be injured. On a scale of one to ten, how would you rate your pain?"

"I think it's about a two right now. Mainly I'm just blue."

Baymax scanned Mike. "The patient is stable but in need of a hug." He grabbed Mike in a powerful hug, then put him down.

"Nice work," said Aladdin. "Let's go! Destination: Cave of Wonders."

"Wait," said Jasmine. "My father once told me of a cursed treasure buried deep in a dungeon."

"So?" said Mike, frowning. "I have been attacked by pirates. Chased by Palace Guards. Kidnapped and held prisoner. Attacked by Stitch—whatever he is! I'm not giving up! I'm a captain, and as captain, I'm going to get *my* treasure!"

"I'm with ya!" said Merida.

"Count me in," said Jack.

"I'm not afraid of the curse," said Aladdin. Jasmine quickly nodded in agreement. She wasn't afraid, either.

"I'm here for you, buddy," said Sulley.

"Then it's settled," said Mike. "We go to the Cave of Wonders, get the treasure—and with our new buddies here, we might have a chance."

"This plan sounds dangerous," Baymax said. "I cannot recommend it for optimal health—"

"But count us in," Hiro finished.

They boarded Baymax and flew

over the jungle and the lava beds, back to the Cave of Wonders. High up in the sky, safe on Baymax, they knew their biggest challenge was still ahead.

Baymax glided to a stop near the entrance to the cave by the tiger's head. They went down the stairs and into the tunnel. There was no sign of Davy or Randy or the hammer-headed guy, whose name was Macchus.

With Baymax's help, they smashed through a locked door and found some weapons—blunderbusses, axes, paintball guns, swords, and a flamingo-shaped croquet mallet. *Now* they were ready to find the treasure . . . and fight.

As they crept along, Merida saw something move above her. It was Randy flying down into the tunnel on a glider.

"Let's finish this!" the little monster said. He was wielding a flintlock.

Merida fought back. Mike joined in her brawl with Randy.

"This is *my* treasure, Randy," said Mike. "You can't win this one!"

Mike blasted Randy with a paintball gun. The villainous little monster lost his balance and rolled toward the lava beds. Baymax swooped down in time, rescuing Randy from the hot goo.

With Randy held firmly in his rocket

fist, Baymax dropped him into a churning pit of tar and mud. "Chances of survival now greatly improved," said Baymax.

"Good save!" yelled Mike. "Too bad he's a bad guy."

"It is not in my programming to allow harm to come to any type of guy," said Baymax.

With Randy down for the moment, Mike, Merida, Sulley, Aladdin, and Baymax ran into the Cave of Wonders, looking for Davy. They found Macchus guarding the entrance to the tunnels.

Baymax used his rocket fist on Macchus. It shot the monstrous pirate all

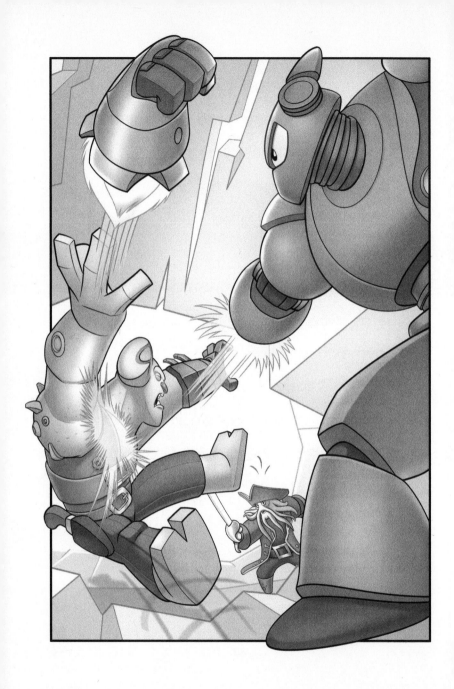

the way down the tunnel.

As the rocket fist returned, it smashed into Davy. Baymax had knocked out both Macchus and Davy with one punch!

"They will sleep now," said Baymax.

They had stopped Davy from loading the weapons and bars of gold onto his elephant's back.

"My treasure!" said Mike. He picked up one of the gold bars. "Hey, I would have thought gold would be heavier." He scratched the bar, and the gold flaked off. "This is *fake gold*!"

"That can't be the real treasure," said Jack. "We have to keep looking."

Aladdin and Merida tied the bad guys together. Baymax lifted Davy and Macchus and placed them on the elephant's back.

As soon as they were ready, Mike said, "Let's go find the *real* treasure."

Chapter 8

They spread the map on the floor of the tunnel and fit both pieces together. Jasmine and Merida read the map.

"I know the answer is here somewhere," Merida said.

"But where? There are hundreds

of rooms and dozens of tunnels. We'd have to blast this whole thing wide open—"

"We can't do that," said Aladdin. "There are strange powers here. It would be terrible luck for us to destroy the Cave of Wonders."

"We're missing something . . . ," said Mike. He looked down and a tiny beetle scampered over his foot. "The scarab! We need both halves of the mystical beetle. Quick! We have to get it from Randy."

They ran over to the elephant. Davy Jones and Randy were not happy.

"*You* don't have the beetle, do you?"

said Randy smugly to Mike.

"You guys have lost," Mike said. "We have it all!"

"Except for the beetle—see what I mean, *partner*?"

"Oh, I get it," replied Mike. "You want in now, after all this?"

Mike realized that he and his friends needed Randy and his half of the beetle. He untied Randy.

"All right, let's get this treasure . . . *together,*" Mike said with a sigh.

Randy reached over to Davy Jones and pulled the beetle from under one of his tentacles. "Right where I left it."

Davy Jones growled at him.

Mike and Randy went back to the map and put the beetle on it. Nothing happened.

"Where's the treasure?" said Mike.

"I don't get it," said Randy.

"Maybe it needs you to say something," Merida interrupted excitedly. "Like an enchanted word?"

"Like 'abracadabra'?" said Jasmine.

"Or something like 'Agrabah'!" said Merida.

"'Agrabah'?" said Jasmine.

"'Agrabah,'" said Mike. "Why not?"

Just then, the tunnel walls started to shake.

"Look!" said Jack.

The wall began to split.

"Of course!" Jasmine said. "We just said 'Agrabah' three times in a row. That must be the magic phrase!"

"It's a treasure *room*!" said Mike. "A whole room!"

Everybody ran over to the opening in the wall. Beyond it was a wide room filled with gleaming vehicles. Race cars, motorcycles, Cinderella's carriage, a hovercraft, bicycles, gliders, four-wheelers, and more. Shiny, colorful, powered up, and ready to race!

"What is this, a *garage*? Where's the gold, the rubies, the diamonds?" Mike sat down glumly. "I'm getting the

feeling there is no real treasure."

"Maybe this *is* the treasure, old buddy," said Sulley. "Look at all these cool race cars, right? You love cars."

"I guess," said Mike.

"Come on—this is fun!" said Hiro.

Everyone boarded a vehicle, and the room began to sparkle. A ramp appeared, leading to a long racetrack that stretched farther than they could see. They all rode their vehicles onto the track, which included an obstacle course, with bars to jump over and hoops of fire to leap through. The track curved into the sky. They stopped to see how far up it went.

"Oooh!" said Merida. "How Angus and I would love to run on that!"

At the mention of her horse's name, she heard a whinny. Angus trotted over and snorted in agreement. He *would* like to race on that track.

They looked up at all the amazing twists and turns. But just then, Hiro saw a shooting star.

"Look, Baymax," he said. "That's the star we came here on."

"Our departure is imminent," said Baymax. "Goodbye."

They all said goodbye to their super-hero friends.

"Aladdin!" Jasmine called out,

feeling the pull of her own shooting star. He grabbed her hand. "To Agrabah. Goodbye, everyone!"

"Wow, people come and go so quickly around here," said Mike.

"We're up next," said Sulley.

"Aw, shucks," said Mike. "I wanted treasure, and I got nothing but a bunch of really great friends. Hey, wait a second! All my new friends . . . Could *that* be the treasure? Okay! I'm good!"

That left Merida and Jack. "I'd love to race here," said Merida. "But my mother and father will be waiting for us with dinner. So Angus and I had best be off to Scotland."

"With these stars, you never know what fate awaits you," said Jack. "It's been a pleasure." He bowed. "To happy adventures." And with that, he was gone in a sparkling twirl of magical dust.

"Bye, Jack!" she shouted. "Well, it's just us, Angus. What do you say we try out this track a bit before we go?"

Just then, the sky lit up and another star streaked across the heavens. Pink sparkles swirled in the air. A girl with long blond hair in a royal blue dress appeared. She zoomed past Merida, skating on ice. Snow flew from beneath her feet!

"Whoa! She has the look of an ice princess—the kind who races!"

Behind Princess Elsa was a large bulky man in a red suit who rode a hoverboard.

"He looks incredible! Who *are* these curious folk?" she asked. "I can't wait to find out! Let's follow them, Angus."

Forgetting dinner, she nudged her horse. Off they went, racing down the track, following Elsa and Mr. Incredible.

THE END?

COMING SOON!

Disney Infinity Chapter Book #3

ICE RACE!

ISBN 978-0-7364-3424-9

Disney Infinity is an action-packed video game featuring a mix of characters as wide-ranging as Elsa from Disney *Frozen,* Merida from Disney/ Pixar *Brave,* and Jack Sparrow from Disney *Pirates of the Caribbean.* Boys and girls will love this *Disney Infinity* chapter-book series, which combines the action and humor from the hit game. In *Ice Race,* Elsa and her friends challenge each other to see who can make the most amazing obstacle course! The possibilities for fun are endless!